Happ

Love from Veronica &
Gordon
xx

Published by Ladybird Books Ltd
80 Strand London WC2R 0RL
A Penguin Company
13 15 17 19 20 18 16 14
© Ladybird Books Ltd MCMXCIX

LADYBIRD and the device of a Ladybird are
trademarks of Ladybird Books Ltd

© Disney MCMXCIX

Based on the Pooh stories by A A Milne
(copyright The Pooh Properties Trust)

Printed in Italy

Disney's

Winnie the Pooh

The Most Grand Adventure

On the very last day of a glorious summer, Christopher Robin said to Pooh, "I have something to tell you."

"Is it something good?" asked Pooh.

"Not exactly," said Christopher Robin.

"Then it can wait," said Pooh. "Because today is only for good things."

Pooh and Christopher Robin went off
exploring. As they ran through the
forest, Pooh suddenly spotted a honey
cave. He picked up a jar of honey, but
the bees in the cave woke up, and
buzzed angrily.

"Quick," said Christopher Robin.
"To the river!" And soon they were
safe on their raft.

"I love being with you, we have such
nice adventures," said Pooh.

"Even when we're apart, we'll always
be together in our hearts," said
Christopher Robin, hugging his friend.

The next morning Pooh woke to the first day of autumn. "Today is a good day for visiting my friends," he thought.

The first thing he saw outside was a lonely pot of honey. "Who does this belong to?" he wondered. "I know, I'll ask Christopher Robin." But his friend was nowhere to be seen. "Perhaps he's visiting Piglet," Pooh thought. And he set off for Piglet's house, taking the honey pot with him.

Pooh found Piglet swinging from a branch at the top of the tree. He was collecting acorns – and they kept falling on Pooh's head! Then Piglet suddenly squealed, "Help! Get me down!" The branch had cracked! "Fetch Christopher Robin!" cried Piglet.

"I can't find him," called Pooh.

Luckily Tigger turned up just at that moment, and said, "My tail has unlimited bounce – I'll rescue Piglet." And he did. But Tigger's bouncing knocked the tree and hundreds of acorns tumbled down on the friends.

Pooh, Piglet and Tigger ran for the safety of Rabbit's house. But to Pooh's surprise, Christopher Robin wasn't there. They hurried to Eeyore's house but Christopher Robin wasn't there either. Pooh told them all about the mysterious pot of honey. Rabbit looked at it and said, "There's a note on it. Let's take it to Owl. He can read anything."

Owl peered at the note and said, "Christopher Robin has gone to SKULL. You must rescue him."

"But how do we know where that is?" asked Pooh.

"I have a map," said Owl. "All you have to do is follow the marked path." Then he added, "There may be monsters." He gave the map to Pooh, saying, "Good luck!"

So Pooh, Piglet, Tigger, Rabbit and Eeyore set off to rescue Christopher Robin. Soon tall trees surrounded them and a big rock appeared in their path. "That rock isn't on the map," said Pooh, worried.

"You're lost!" said Rabbit, grabbing the map from him. But as he spoke, they heard a deep GROWL.

"A monster!" cried Piglet, running off as fast as he could, the others close behind.

Piglet ran out of the forest and found himself in a valley full of butterflies. They fluttered around him, then picked him up. Piglet was frightened. But Pooh came to his rescue. He leapt as high as he could, grabbed Piglet, and hung on. It was too much for the butterflies. They dropped Pooh and Piglet into a bed of flowers, then flew away.

"That was brave, Pooh," said Piglet. And off they went again.

But they still couldn't find Christopher Robin. Then the wind blew away a bit of the map, and Tigger had to run to get it back. By this time they were all getting rather tired. "It's no good," said Rabbit. "I don't know where we are."

Pooh peered through the mist. "Let's rest in that cave over there," he said.

"Look! THIS is where the map was leading us," said Rabbit as they went into the cave. "Christopher Robin is in here!" So Pooh wandered away by himself to find Christopher Robin.

It was very cold, and there were ice crystals everywhere. Then Tigger saw Pooh through the ice crystals – he looked ENORMOUS. "Run!" yelled Tigger, frightened. "It's an ice monster!"

Pooh heard Tigger shout, but he didn't know why. In his panic, he slipped down to the bottom of a deep, deep hole – still holding his pot of honey. All of a sudden, CLUNK, there was another big pot there as well. When Pooh investigated, he found it was full of honey. And he fell in!

Christopher Robin had lowered the big pot of honey to rescue Pooh! He pulled up his friend, laughing.

"But what did the honey and the note mean?" asked Pooh, puzzled.

"The honey was for you," said Christopher Robin. "The note said it was my first day at school. I'm going again tomorrow."

"But will we always be together?" asked Pooh.

"For ever and ever!" smiled Christopher Robin, giving Pooh a big hug.

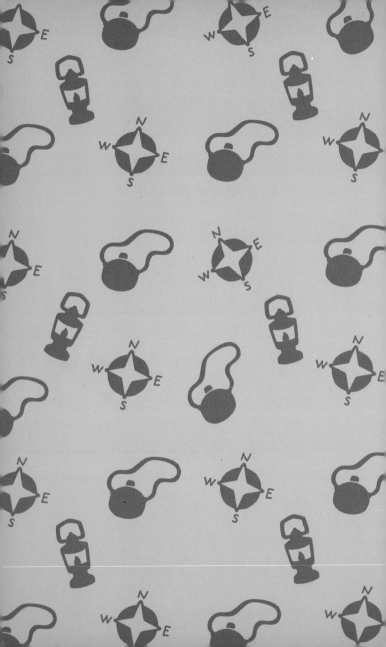